Pirates for Parrots

By Anna Maria Sophia Cancelli

Pirates for Parrots

Copyright © 2018 Cape Fear Parrot Sanctuary

Photo credits: Photographs provided by Ces Erdman, Bo Bauer, Corey Lefkowitz, and Anna Maria Sophia Cancelli.

ISBN: 9781728700823

Dedication

This story is dedicated to two very special parrots, Logan and Charlie the Picasso of Parrots. Logan, one of the Cape Fear Parrot Sanctuary educational birds, was a cockatiel who after 22 years took flight to the heavens. Charlie the Picasso of Parrots is an eclectus in his 60s who paints on canvas and sells his masterpieces to raise funds for Cape Fear Parrot Sanctuary residents. Charlie is a sweet and loving parrot who habitually plucks out his own feathers. Despite the fact that he is a feather plucker and looks different from most parrots, he is still beautiful and loved by all who meet him.

Acknowledgments

I wish to acknowledge and thank Cape Fear Parrot Sanctuary
esident Ces Erdman, Alan Smith, Charlie the Picasso of Parrots, and my
ate friends for making this story possible.

Table of Contents

Chapter 1

Sunny's Grand Adventure

On a bright, warm afternoon deep in the heart of a rain forest, Sunny and Logan hopped from branch to branch, climbing high up a tree on a journey to see what lay beyond the thick **foliage**. Sunny, a bright yellow sun **conure**, and his friend Logan, a **cockatiel**, were on a grand adventure. Being young boys, the two played high in a tree pretending to be explorers on a **quest** for new lands.

"I spy a ship!" Sunny shouted.

"Where? Where? Let me see," urged Logan, pushing Sunny aside he could peek through the leaves.

"Look toward the **horizon**," Sunny replied.

Lowering his wings in disappointment, Logan turned to Sunny and said, "There's no ship out there."

"Yes there is!" Sunny **gleefully** replied. "It's beyond the horizon We just can't see it yet."

The two friends sat in silence **peering** out through the leaves, **squinting** their eyes tighter and tighter hoping to catch a **glimpse** of a **topsail**.

"Boys, it's time to come home. The sun is setting," hollered Sunny's mom from a distance.

Without **hesitation**, Sunny and Logan flew home to the safety of their families. They knew that tomorrow would bring another opportunity for exploration and adventure.

Just as soon as the sun came up the next day, Sunny and Logan were up in a tree pretending to be explorers again. They fashioned flow

tals into helmets because they believed no self-respecting explorer would
ɪbark on a journey without a helmet for protection. The two boys
ɪrched dozens of trees for the perfect **perch** from which they could
ve an **unobstructed** view of the sea. After finding the perfect perch,
ɪy turned their **gaze** to the ocean and hoped that a ship would come
o view.

"Sunny, what do we do if we actually see a ship?" Logan asked.

"Well, if it's close to shore, we should try to fly out to it," Sunny
ɔughtfully replied.

"What? Why would we fly out to a ship without even knowing who
what is on it?" Logan asked.

"Because we are on an adventure," Sunny responded.

"But Sunny, we're just pretending to be explorers. We can't just fly
ɔard a boat we know nothing about. It might be dangerous," Logan
ɔlained.

In a most serious tone Sunny declared, "I want a real adventure. I
ɪt to go on a **voyage**. I am tired of being stuck here in the forest. I want
ɪee what else the world has to offer."

Logan, always being the voice of reason, responded by saying,
ɪnny, you can't just leave your family and friends. Parrots live in **flocks**.
ɪ world outside of the forest may not be a safe place if you are all
ɪe."

"Safety schmafety," said Sunny. "I'm young, and I want to go on an
ɪenture."

Logan flapped his wings in disagreement and hoped that a ship
ɪld never come into sight.

All of a sudden, the bright sun **illuminated** something moving on
ɪsea.

2

"A ship!" screamed Sunny. "I see a ship. See it, Logan?"

"Yes," answered his friend in a very disappointed tone. "Yes. I see a ship."

Spreading his wings as wide as he could, Sunny flew out of the tree across the beach, and toward the ocean. The ship was close to shore, so Sunny reached it in no time at all and circled it a time or two.

A few of the sailors aboard the **sloop** noticed Sunny and **curiously observed** as he flew around the topsail. Seeing that he had the attention of the sailors, Sunny **swooped** in and flew above their heads.

"**Avast, mates**," one of the sailors called. "Look at that mighty fine bird trying to get our attention."

"A mighty fine bird **indeed**," commented another sailor.

"What a fine companion he would make," yet another sailor said.

All the sailors then began to laugh. Sunny took this as a sign that the men aboard this ship were a friendly bunch, so he swooped in low and perched atop one of their shoulders. This **amused** the men, who laughed even more, making Sunny very happy, so happy that he didn't give any thought to returning home that day and instead stayed aboard the ship until after sunset.

Logan waited for Sunny as long as he could, then flew home once the sun went down.

"Help! Help! Pirates have abducted Sunny," screamed Logan as he landed on his family's tree.

"Logan, stop telling tales," cautioned his mother.

"Mom, it's not a tale. Sunny and I were pretending to be explorers when we saw a ship sailing close to shore. Sunny flew out to it, and now the ship is out to sea with Sunny on board! Mom, we have to help," Logan urged.

Logan's mother tried to calm him down by telling him that Sunny isn't gone for good and would soon fly home. Logan explained that nny wanted an adventure and was eager to go on a voyage. Since Sunny w off while the sun was still high in the sky and had not returned by nset, Logan's mother decided to form a search party.

All the birds in the village flew to the shore in search of Sunny, but ship could be seen on the sea. When asked what the ship looked like, only detail Logan could remember was the black flag with skull and ossbones flying from the main **mast**.

"Pirates!" Sunny's mother **shrieked**. "My darling son has been ducted by pirates!"

"He wasn't abducted," Logan stated. "He wanted to go on an enture."

Sunny's mother cried. She refused to believe her son was gone for od and insisted that the search party find him and bring him home. ny's mother knew exactly who needed to lead the **expedition**: Charlie Picasso of Parrots!

Chapter 2

Charlie the Picasso of Parrots

Charlie spent his days painting. He was an **eclectus** with a bright green head and a pleasing personality. Everyone liked him even though he had few feathers. He was different from all the other parrots in the village but he was well liked and respected because he was talented and kind. Once he heard about Sunny disappearing with **brigands**, he was eager to help find the boy bird and bring him home.

Under the **cloak** of darkness, Sunny's mom, Charlie, Logan, and flock of parrots from the village made their way to the other side of the forest to a bay where they knew ships sometimes docked. One ship was the bay, but it was not flying the flag Logan said he saw on the sloop that took Sunny away.

Charlie gathered all the parrots together to discuss their next move. According to Charlie, pirates would keep their identity hidden until they were out on the open sea and ready to strike, and only then would they **hoist** the **Jolly Roger** and use it as a way to **intimidate** those aboard the ship they were planning to **capture**. For that reason, Charlie suggested they wait until nightfall and board the ship in the bay because that **vessel** just might be carrying the pirates Sunny took up with.

As soon as the sun went down and the stars came up, the moon cast a dim glow across the bay. The ship **weighed anchor** and slowly slipped away from the dock.

"Take flight!" announced Charlie.

The parrots took heed of the command and flew aboard the ship which belonged to Captain Dogfish Briggins.

Once aboard the ship, the parrots found safe places to hide while iting for the sailors to fall asleep. The plan was to search for Sunny once last sailor took to his **hammock** for the night.

A **thorough** search **revealed** that Sunny was nowhere to be found this particular pirate ship.

Once morning came, the parrots listened to the sailors' nversations and learned that the ship they were aboard was a pirate ship its way to meet a **plethora** of other pirates somewhere along the rolina coast. The parrots stayed hidden to avoid **detection** so they ld safely travel to the Carolina coast and continue their search for nny.

Charlie was very curious, and even though he should have been ing with the other parrots, he could not help but take a walk on deck t to investigate further.

"Hello," he heard a sweet voice call.

"Hello?" Charlie replied.

"Pleased to meet you," the sweet voice spoke.

When Charlie turned to look in the direction of the voice, he saw a geous **macaw**, the loveliest he had ever seen.

"I'm Tova," the beautiful female parrot announced.

"I'm . . . I'm Charlie," mumbled the eclectus.

"What brings you aboard, Charlie?" Tova asked.

Charlie was a bit tongue-tied at the sight of the beautiful lady bird, he did manage to explain. "My friends and I are trying to track down **wayward** flock member, Sunny, who left on a pirate ship."

"Lucky for you my captain is a friend to parrots," offered Tova. "Once we arrive at our **destination**, we can ask Captain Dogfish Briggin if he would be willing to help."

Charlie felt happy knowing there was a chance Sunny would be found, and his heart filled with joy. He also felt a strong sense of purpose and suddenly felt something he had never ever felt before . . . **smitten**.

Charlie the Picasso of Parrots

Chapter 3

Sunny's New Friends

The journey to Carolina was long and filled with everything from
r winds to foul weather. Captain Dogfish Briggins' ship finally arrived
the Carolina coast not far from the mouth of the Cape Fear River.

The parrots flew ashore and were surprised to see other birds just
them perched in nearby trees. They met a blue and gold macaw named
o Toes Beau who told the forest flock that he had seen a conure as
ght as the sun aboard a ship belonging to Captain **Waylay** Wayne, a
wn pirate.

The flock, along with Two Toes Beau, then flew along the shore,
ere they listened carefully and watched closely, hoping to locate Sunny.

Sunny was with Captain Waylay Wayne, who was in a shop
ghing it up with a **merchant** while **negotiating** the price of a wheel of
ese. Sunny was perched atop Captain Waylay Wayne's shoulder, helping
count coins to pay for the cheese.

Sunny had never seen **currency** before, and he didn't understand
the pirates found it so important.

"**Ye** can buy food, and ye can buy drink, and just to have a little of
akes a person feel **superior**," Captain Waylay explained.

"What does it mean to be superior?" Sunny asked.

"Ye see," Captain Waylay said, "some of us were not born with
lth, and because of that we be looked down upon. But to have money
e pocket makes me feel like I am just as good as those who are rich."

This confused Sunny because he never knew his family or friends
ink they were better than other parrots. He then flew off and helped a
pirate named Rusty Buckles collect little jewels hidden in the sand.

8

"What is so important about collecting jewels?" Sunny asked Rust

"**'Tis** fun," Rusty replied.

Sunny didn't understand that either, because when he was home i the forest the only thing he needed for fun was a tree to climb with his friend Logan.

Sunny felt sad when he thought of Logan. He felt even more sad when he thought of his mother and the other parrots in his village. He realized that he was the only parrot among all the pirates, and that made him feel lonely. He liked his new pirate friends, but he missed his forest friends and his family.

That night before going to sleep, Sunny wished that he would be able to see his friend Logan and his family again soon.

The following morning, the sound of a voice barking orders wok Sunny. He opened his eyes and flew down to the deck where all the pira were **furiously** working on making the ship ready for **departure**.

"What's going on?" Sunny asked Captain Waylay Wayne.

"The **Governor**'s men are after us," Captain Waylay Wayne repli "They say the coins and jewels we have do not belong to us. Surely we be punished if they catch us! We must weigh anchor and **set sail!**"

Captain Waylay Wayne and his crew left in a hurry and sailed alo the Carolina coast into the Cape Fear River in an attempt to escape from the Governor's men. Captain Waylay Wayne knew that once he made it through the mouth of the river he would be able to sail inland, find a waterway to hide in, and return to sea once the coast was clear.

Rusty Buckles

Chapter 4

Parrots of the Cape Fear

Upon receiving word that Captain Waylay Wayne, his crewmemb Rusty Buckles, and a bright yellow conure left **port** in a hurry to escape capture, Charlie and the flock flew back to the ship belonging to Captain Dogfish Briggins.

"I have a plan!" announced Charlie. "I am sure Captain Briggins a reasonable man, so let's ask him if he will take us for a ride up the Cap Fear. Certainly he won't turn down our request, especially if Tova will le us to him."

"Follow me!" called Tova, leading the flock to her captain.

Initially, Captain Dogfish Briggins was not interested in taking orders from a flock of parrots.

"I will do no such thing!" Captain Dogfish Briggins said in response to Charlie's request. "I am a captain. I make the orders, not tal the orders. Besides, there is no good reason for me to sail up the Cape Fear."

"Captain Briggins!" hollered Bo the **bosun**. "The Governor's me are searching for pirates! No one must leave the ship! We must **cast off** immediately or surely we will be punished!"

Captain Dogfish Briggins turned to Tova and the other parrots a said, "Well now, I believe we will indeed be taking a trip up the Cape F after all. The winds be fair, so let's cast off and find **yer** fine feathered friend Sunny."

When the ship entered the Cape Fear River, the parrots were amazed at how much the lands on each side of the river looked like the

11

rest they called home. They were also surprised that so many birds of ery type could be seen flying between the trees that lined the riverbank.

"Avast! Pirate ship ahead!" shouted one of the pirates who had en keeping watch through a **spyglass**.

Upon that announcement, the parrots took to the sky, flapping ir wings as fast as they could to catch up to the ship ahead of them.

Captain Dogfish Briggins' ship soon dropped anchor alongside the op belonging to Captain Waylay Wayne. Side by side, the two ships ated silently.

"**Ahoy**!" called Captain Dogfish Briggins. "Ahoy, I say!"

"Ahoy!" Captain Waylay Wayne called back.

"I understand ye have a parrot on board named Sunny. His family friends are looking for him," hollered Captain Dogfish Briggins.

"Ah yes," replied Captain Waylay Wayne. "A plethora of parrots boarded and are reuniting with young Sunny."

"Very well indeed," replied Captain Dogfish Briggins. "May I be wed to board?"

"**Aye**," replied Captain Waylay Wayne. "Aye."

As the birds celebrated, the two captains stood face to face, looking piciously at each other.

"Perhaps if ye give me some of yer coins and jewels I will let ye and crew sail away unharmed," offered Captain Dogfish Briggins.

"Perhaps if ye and yer birds get off me ship I will make sure ye and crew do not sink to the bottom of this river!" Captain Waylay Wayne ited in reply.

"What is going here?" Charlie asked. "There's no reason to fight. And there certainly is no reason to take something that does not belong to you, Captain Briggins!"

"He took it from someone else," Captain Dogfish Briggins replied. "I have just as much a right to it as he does."

"This makes no sense," Charlie replied. Charlie could not understand why the two captains were so interested in coins and jewels. He also did not understand how either captain could feel he had a right to things that did not belong to either of them.

Because the parrots were busy reuniting with Sunny, and because the two captains were involved in an **altercation**, no one noticed the third ship sail up.

"Avast!" called an officer standing on deck of the third ship. "We are here on behalf of the Governor. All pirates will be taken captive and will be punished!"

"Oh no!" cried Logan. "How will we all get home?"

"Yes, how are these birds going to get home?" Captain Waylay Wayne asked the officer. "Surely ye will leave me be so that I may take these parrots back to their forest. It's far too far for them to fly home."

"Excuse me," interrupted Captain Dogfish Briggins, "but I carried the **majority** of the parrots to this point, so surely I must be the one to take them all home."

"Now look here," hollered the **leftenant**, "all pirates will be punished for crimes of **thievery**!"

The pirates were then forced to **disembark** their ships and board the Governor's ship.

The parrots flew onto the Governor's ship to find out what fate pirates would meet. Even parrots perched in trees along the Cape Fear

ver flew down and landed on the deck of the Governor's ship to see
hat would happen.

Tova decided to be friendly and greeted the Cape Fear parrots.

"Hello. I am Sinbad. Pleased to meet you," a yellow-naped **amazon**
plied. "I was **poached** from my homeland, brought here to Carolina
ere I was sold, but I outlived my owner, and now I live here along the
pe Fear River in the trees."

"Hello. I am Bella," said a lovely little cockatiel. "I was a present for
ttle girl, but I was too much for her to take care of, so now I live in a
e on the bank of this river."

One by one, the Cape Fear parrots came forward, introduced
mselves, and told their sad tales. They had all lost their owners or their
nes and had come together and created a community in the trees that
dered the Cape Fear River. All the pirates and all the Governor's men
od on deck watching the Cape Fear birds tell their sad tales. There was
a dry eye aboard the ship.

"I have a plan," said the leftenant. "What if we get the Governor
ardon the pirates? And what if the conditions of that pardon include
ning over a new leaf, so rather than taking things, the pirates give back
ead?"

A hush fell over the Cape Fear.

"What if," continued the leftenant, "what if the pirates gave back
oh . . . say . . . building a proper home for all these parrots and helping
care of them?"

Everyone remained silent . . .

But then . . .

"**Huzzah**!" shouted Rusty Buckles. "Why, I think that is a fine idea! I, for one, would enjoy helping provide for these fine feathered creatures!"

"Indeed!" cheered Captain Dogfish Briggins. "I **concur**, and I too would be pleased to be of service to these beautiful birds!"

"I'm ready to build **aviaries**! Who's with me?" asked Captain Waylay Wayne.

All the pirates and all the parrots cheered wildly!

"But what about us?" asked Charlie. "How are we going to get back home to the rain forest?"

"I have an idea!" shouted Logan. "I have a plan for all of us to have an adventure AND to help our Cape Fear friends."

Sunny was amazed. In all the years he had been friends with Logan, he had seen him as a follower rather than a leader. He also knew that Logan was afraid to try new things, and now he spoke of adventure! What a day! He couldn't wait to hear what Logan had to say.

"I propose," continued Logan, "that all of us from the rain forest help our Cape Fear friends get settled in to their new home and stay to experience new things."

Charlie spoke up and said, "I think Logan has a fine idea, a fine idea indeed. Just like we were all willing to help find Sunny when he went off on his little adventure, so should we help our Cape Fear friends now that they are in need."

All the pirates and all the parrots cheered wildly!

And so began another adventure for pirates and parrots. They would travel up the Cape Fear River to find the perfect place to build a **sanctuary** where parrots would live in safety and **serenity** and be taken care of by their pirate friends.

Bo the Bosun

Chapter 5

Curse of the Sea Witch

On a warm summer afternoon, parrots flapped their wings in joy pirates sang sea **shanties** while working away at the Cape Fear Parrot Sanctuary not far from the Cape Fear River.

"Yo ho, yo ho," the pirates sang.

"Yo ho, yo ho," the parrots replied.

The pirates were happy because they had not been punished for being thieves. They had received pardons in exchange for giving back instead of taking. The pirates decided that instead of committing crimes the high seas, they would care for their parrot friends.

On this particular day, the pirates were hard at work building aviaries and harvesting the fruits and vegetables they grew in the sanctua garden.

Rusty Buckles, the lady pirate, was in charge of the garden. She v skilled at growing a variety of vegetables and made sure there was alway enough food for the parrots and the pirates to eat.

Bo the bosun helped collect apples by climbing up a tree and tossing the fruit into a large basket below.

"These be some mighty fine apples," hollered the bosun from hi up in the tree. "Sure would be nice if someone would make a pie."

Rusty pretended not to hear the bosun and continued plucking green beans from the vine.

"An apple pie most certainly would be wonderful," Bo the bosu hollered again.

"Aye, aye," Rusty Buckles replied. "I will make an apple pie for ssert. Yes indeed."

The bosun smiled and was thankful that a he had a **delectable** ssert to look forward to after a day of hard work.

Once the sun set and all the parrots and all the pirates had their ning meal, Rusty Buckles brought a hot apple pie to the table. Rusty ok out her trusty blade and cut the pie into pieces, making sure that each ate received an equal share.

"Rusty, how did ye learn to grow such wonderful fruits and getables and make such delicious pies?" asked Bo the bosun.

"Before becoming a pirate, I had a farm," Rusty replied. "I also had usband, and I made apple pies for him."

"A farm and a husband!" howled the bosun.

"Aye. A farm and a husband," Rusty responded as her smile ppeared.

"I didn't mean to make ye sad, Rusty," the bosun said. "I am ry."

"No worries, mate. It was a long time ago," Rusty answered.

A **multitude** of stars were out on this warm summer night, with y a cloud in the sky. The gentle evening breeze reminded Rusty of her on the farm.

"My name was Charlotte back then," the lady pirate said. "My band, Jonathan, and I were farmers in Ireland. We were tired of **toiling** y to make the landlord rich and spending all our hard earned money on , so we decided to travel to the **colonies** to start a farm of our own."

"Sounds smart," said Charlie, who was sharing a piece of pie with a te.

18

"'**Twas**," replied Rusty. "It most certainly was . . . until we were cursed by the sea witch and Jonathan was taken away from me."

Rusty could see by the look on the pirates' faces that they were eager to hear more.

"A **torrential** storm was **aloft** the night Jonathan and I were to depart Ireland for the New World. It was our only opportunity to leave, and we knew that if we did not board the ship that very night we would miss our chance to start a new life. The ship tossed about on the ocean while a **tempest** raged. We all feared we would lose our lives."

The pirates all sighed heavily.

"We knew there was only one way to calm the raging sea," said Rusty. "We had to call upon the sea witch and **entreat** her to deliver us safely."

"Confront the sea witch? That be dangerous!" shouted Bo the bosun.

"True. Very true," Rusty confirmed. "At my urging, Jonathan sto on the **bow** of the boat and called to the sea witch. He promised that w would pay her a portion of our wealth once our farm began to **prosper** exchange for safe passage to the New World. As soon as that **vow** was made, the wind died down, the sea became calm, the clouds parted, and the dark night gave way to a million stars and a bright moon that lit the way to the New World. And we arrived safely."

The pirates and the parrots were pleased to see a smile return to Rusty's face. But that smile was short-lived.

"We had a lovely little farm, and we did become rich, but not ric with money. We were rich because we had friends and made the town f happy by selling the most flavorful fruits and vegetables in the land. We were rich in fellowship, which is much better than being rich in money.

"Sounds lovely," sighed Bo the Bosun.

"'Twas," Rusty responded. "'Twas indeed . . . until the sea witch
me to collect. It was very cold the night the sea witch showed up. That
rticular winter was **harsh**, and the fall harvest was not as **profitable** as
had hoped. We had been able to purchase a few necessary **provisions**
winter such as bread and butter, but we had little else. Jonathan and I
re sitting in front of a warm fire when we heard a knock at the door.
nathan opened the door, and there in the cold night air stood a cloaked
man. Neither Jonathan nor I recognized her, but when she insisted that
must make good on our promise to pay, we knew exactly who she
s."

"Was it the sea witch?" asked Charlie.

"'Twas indeed," Rusty replied. "There stood Mara Strega, witch of
sea, reminding us of how we arrived in the colonies. She spoke of the
rm we sailed into the night we left for the New World and how my
oved Jonathan stood on the bow of the ship calling to her for help. She
come to collect what we owed her, but we were unable to pay."

The pirates felt sad listening to Rusty Buckles tell her tale. It broke
r hearts to find out that the sea witch cursed the couple and placed a
l on Jonathan, making him disappear into the night.

"The sea witch then told me that money would no longer be good
ugh, and the only way to pay our **debt** was to give her a chest full of
els," Rusty said. "So I left my farm and went in search of jewels so that
uld get my beloved Jonathan back. I wasn't sure where to look, but I
heard stories about pirates returning from sea with trunks filled with
sure, so I thought the seashore would be a fine place to start."

"Pirates have treasure. Pirates have treasure," called out Two Toes
u.

"Aye," Rusty replied. "After nearly a year of **combing** the beach, I
cted enough jewels to fill a chest. Of course, spending so much time

on the shore looking for jewels rusted the buckles on my shoes. That is when I was given the name Rusty Buckles."

A smile appeared on Rusty's face once again. That smile made all the other pirates smile.

"Perhaps we need to help our good mate Rusty Buckles find the witch so the curse can be removed," suggested Charlie.

"A fine idea indeed!" shouted Bo the bosun. "I will ask the captai if in the **morn** we can prepare to cast off."

The pirates turned in for the night, as they surely needed a good night's sleep before such an important journey.

Charlie and Tova made their way to a perch.

"You look so very lovely tonight, Tova," Charlie said.

"Oh, Charlie, you **flatter** me," Tova said with a smile. "I really lil that you are an artist," she added. "I think you are the most talented par I have ever met."

"Thank you," Charlie replied.

"How did you become a painter?" The lady bird asked.

"Well," Charlie said, "it began many years ago when I became curious about a ship in the bay and flew aboard to take a look. A sailor dropped a sail next to a few jars of paint on the deck. A large wave rock the ship and caused paint to spill on the sail. I was flung off the **yardar** was perched on and fell onto the sail and smeared paint all over it while trying to hop off. The sailor picked up the sail and declared it a mighty piece of artwork, and from then on I was known as Charlie the Picasso Parrots."

Charlie was the most talented bird Tova had ever met. She was impressed with his ability to paint. She also knew he had a big heart because he was always willing help others. She did not mind that he wa

21

ssing feathers because he had a habit of plucking them out and looked
ferent than most of the parrots. She only saw his talent, his bravery, and
kindness.

"I'm a bit cold," said Tova.

"There is a chill in the air," Charlie confirmed, **oblivious** to the fact
t Tova wanted to snuggle.

"Charlie, would you mind coming a bit closer to keep me warm?"
va asked.

Charlie scooted closer to Tova, so close that he felt the beat of her
rt.

"Tova, I like you. I really like you," Charlie said with a smile on his
.

Tova rubbed her beak against Charlie's cheek. This pleased Charlie.
the first time ever, he felt proud to be who he was: a talented, brave,
kind parrot. His lack of feathers did not matter to Tova. She liked
rlie for who he was, and that made Charlie very proud.

Chapter 6

Journey to the Crystal Coast

The rising of the morning sun brought yet another opportunity fo pirates and parrots to embark on a journey together. According to **scuttlebutt**, the sea witch lived somewhere along the Crystal Coast, so pirates and parrots set sail and cast off to help their friend Rusty Buckles find Mara Strega, the sea witch.

After a long voyage, one of the pirates hollered, "**Land ho!**"

"Hand me the spyglass," requested Captain Waylay Wayne who took a look for himself. Sure enough, the land straight ahead was indeed the Crystal Coast.

A search party was formed, and Rusty Buckles rowed the group shore in a **skiff**.

The search party walked a long distance before coming across a small shack surrounded by trees. A large, bright, heart-shaped object wa hanging from one of the trees. A long crack ran through the middle of heart. Clearly, this heart had been broken.

The shack was surrounded by cats. Some cats were stretched ou sunning themselves. Other cats roamed as if they were in search of something, and other cats chased bugs. While most of the cats ignored pirates and parrots, a large black cat with bright green eyes paid close attention to what the **invaders** were doing.

"Hello, kitty," Rusty said to the black cat.

"Greetings, furry friend," said Two Toes Beau.

The cat remained quiet but continued to pay close attention to invaders.

Rusty looked around and noticed a large black **cauldron**.

"A black cat and a cauldron. This must be where the sea witch es," Rusty announced.

"Is this the home of Mara Strega?" Rusty asked the cat.

"Maybe. Why do you want to know?" the cat replied.

"We have a gift for her," answered Rusty Buckles.

"A gift? What sort of gift?" asked the cat.

Rusty Buckles lifted the lid to the chest she was carrying and ealed a **trove** of **gleaming** jewels.

"Now why would you want to give all those colorful rocks to Mara ga?" asked the cat.

"I owe them to her," Rusty replied.

The cat studied the box of jewels before speaking. "Yes. This is the ne of Mara Strega, but she is not here right now. You may leave the of pretty rocks with me. I will make sure she gets it."

"We can't do that," Rusty said. "While I am here to pay my debt, a Strega has something she needs to give me in return. We will wait."

"Suit yourself," the cat replied and then wandered away.

Charlie became curious about something. "Rusty, when the curse is l, will you and Jonathan return to your farm?" he asked the lady pirate.

"I don't know," Rusty replied. "I suppose I will have to talk it over Jonathan. And who knows if that mean old witch will even lift the e. I suppose we won't know until we find her."

Sensing someone approaching, Two Toes Beau began to squawk.

"Who goes there?" Rusty asked.

24

"'Tis I," replied a female voice.

Two Toes Beau began to squawk even louder as a woman approached.

"Good evening," said the woman. "My cat **Onyx** told me that pirates and parrots were looking for me. I am Mara Strega."

Rusty stood in silence studying the small woman standing before her. The woman seemed like any other and not at all like the **notorious** witch Rusty had heard so much about.

"Speak, pirate!" the woman loudly commanded.

"I have a chest filled with jewels for you," Rusty quickly replied. am paying off my debt. I want you to remove the curse and break the sp and return my husband to me."

The sea witch could not believe what she was hearing. She had spent many years roaming the coast casting spells and placing curses, an yet no one had ever actually offered to repay a debt.

"I worked very hard collecting these jewels because it was the pr I had to pay to see my Jonathan again," Rusty said. "Please remove the curse and let him return to me," she begged.

"And how is it that you found me?" the sea witch asked.

"My friends helped me," Rusty replied. "A crew of pirates and a flock of parrots helped me locate you."

The sea witch was touched by Rusty's **devotion** to her husband by the fact that her friends came to her aid when help was needed. Ma Strega was so moved that she decided to let Rusty keep the jewels she worked so hard for.

"Thank you. Thank you so much," Rusty said to the sea witch. will sell the jewels and use the money to help the parrots who live at th Cape Fear Parrot Sanctuary."

The sea witch had not felt happy in many years, but Rusty's joy and generosity made Mara Strega glad.

"So you will remove the curse and bring Jonathan back?" Rusty asked.

Mara Strega put her hands to her heart and said, "My dear girl, I do want to remove the curse and break the spell that keeps your husband far from home. But I cannot."

"What!" **exclaimed** Rusty.

"You see, there was a time when my heart was full of love for my own husband, a sailor named Edward, who was the love of my life. He went to sea and did not return. He was a good man, but he became greedy and turned to piracy. He took a new name and became a **legend**— Blackbeard!"

"What!" Rusty cried out. "You were married to the notorious pirate Blackbeard?"

"Yes," replied the sea witch. "My heart broke when I learned that Edward lost his life. I cannot do anything that involves love until I **mend** my broken heart."

"What can I do to help you repair your broken heart?" Rusty asked the sea witch.

"There is nothing you can do. I must be the one to mend my own broken heart by finding Edward's ghost and letting him know that I forgive him for leaving me and turning to a life of piracy."

"Thank you, Mara Strega," Rusty said **sincerely**.

"Do not thank me yet," replied the sea witch. "Finding Edward's ghost will be difficult to do because his spirit **lingers** along the banks of Ocracoke Island, and I have no boat to **transport** me there."

"I will ask our captains and crew to help," Rusty offered. "Surely we can take you to Ocracoke so you can find and forgive Edward and fe your heart beat again."

The pirates and the parrots were indeed willing to help.

Rusty Buckles sold the jewels she had collected, and Mara Strega took her broken heart down from the tree and placed it inside the empty treasure chest for safekeeping. Everyone was eager to embark on a missi to find Blackbeard's ghost.

Mara Strega the Sea Witch

Chapter 7

Hunt for Blackbeard's Ghost

Rain clouds filled the sky and thunder roared as pirates and parro sailed to Ocracoke Island.

"Can you calm the sea?" Rusty Buckles asked the sea witch.

"I cannot **interfere** with nature on this particular voyage. We mu let the tempest transport us to Ocracoke," Mara Strega replied as a stror current pushed the ship through the rough sea.

Once the storm passed and the clouds parted, a pirate in the **cro nest** shouted, "Land ho!"

Everyone ran to the bow, and all were thrilled to see the island ju ahead.

The parrots flew to shore first, followed by pirates who rowed t shore in skiffs. They set up camp on the beach and began planning the hunt when up the beach came a **formidable** pirate, Commodore Red, a his parrot Rio.

"Aye! Indeed the ghost of Blackbeard has made an appearance the isle of Ocracoke," confirmed Commodore Red. "Nary a night lit b the full moon goes by that we don't see him looking at us through the mist. 'Tis a most frightening sight."

"Tonight the moon will be full," mentioned Rusty Buckles.

"Keep a watchful eye," warned Commodore Red. "Right aroun midnight the full moon will reveal the ghost of Blackbeard, the most feared pirate who ever lived."

"Why did Edward become a pirate?" Rusty asked Mara Strega.

"My Edward was honest and hardworking when we met. We fell in
ve and got married. We made a home for ourselves in my small seaside
lage, but Edward had an **adventuresome** spirit and grew tired of life on
d, so he returned to the sea." Mara Strega spoke with sadness in her
ice. "Edward wanted more out of life than just working hard and having
le. I had a feeling he was up to no good while he was away because he
uld return from trips at sea with things of great value that I knew he
ild not afford, but I had no idea he was a pirate."

"You had no idea that your husband was really the notorious pirate
ckbeard?" Rusty asked.

"No idea at all," the sea witch replied. "Months went by without a
t from Edward. My heart broke once I received word that he died
ause he was a pirate and was doing very bad things. I cried so hard that
heart hardened completely and cracked. I was in so much pain that I
led my broken heart out of my chest and hung it from a tree. From that
forward, I had no heart, and I hurt others so that I wouldn't be alone
ny pain."

"It is never right to hurt others just because you are hurting," Rusty
.

"I know that now," the sea witch replied. "And that is why I must
Edward's ghost. If I can face his ghost and tell him that I forgive him,
ll be relieved of my pain and sorrow, and only then will I be able to
ove the curse."

"**Fer** sure the ghost of Blackbeard will make an appearance at
night under the full moon," confirmed Commodore Red. "First ye will
his shadow. Next ye will see his eyes **ablaze**, glowing red. He steps
y, so ye will hear leaves and twigs crackling beneath his feet, and ye
might feel the earth **tremble**."

Each and every pirate stood wide-eyed in fear.

"Fear ye not," said Commodore Red, "for it is just his spirit ye will encounter. He is not flesh and bone and cannot hurt ye."

"I have never seen a ghost," Sunny said.

"Me neither," Logan said. "I'm terrified!"

"Friends, we have nothing to be afraid of. We are all in this together," said Rusty Buckles. We will keep each other safe. And we have the brave Commodore Red to lead the way. Surely no harm will come to us."

And on that note, the hunt for Blackbeard's ghost began.

Commodore Red lead the way. The group walked alongside a stream under a cloudy, moonless sky. Every now and again a member of the group would become startled if someone stepped on a twig and snapped it.

"Look," Rusty Buckles shouted. "Look! The clouds are parting and the moon is coming out!"

A sudden crashing sound in the distance frightened almost everyone in the group. Pirates breathed deeply, trying to remain calm while parrots flapped their wings in fear. A terrified Rusty Buckles held the treasure chest tightly trying to keep her hands from shaking.

"Who goes there!" shouted Commodore Red.

A large, dark shadow of a man slowly made an appearance.

"Are you friend or **foe**?" asked Mara Strega the sea witch. "Speak specter!" she screamed. "Make yourself known!"

Everyone waited for a reply from the spectral figure, but there was nothing but silence. Suddenly two glowing eyes appeared, and the shadow began floating toward them.

31

"Avast!" hollered Commodore Red. "Be ye the ghost of the torious Blackbeard?"

The dark shadow moved closer and closer until it was directly in nt of them.

"Who seeks me?" the ghostly figure asked in a deep voice.

"'Tis I, Mara Strega," replied the sea witch. "Edward, is that you?"

"I have not been called Edward in many moons," the voice replied.

"Let me see your face, spirit," commanded the sea witch.

The shadow revealed the face of a man. The long, dark beard gave y his identity. It was the ghost of Blackbeard.

All the pirates and all the parrots stood **transfixed**.

The sea witch and the **apparition** stood face to face. She was king deeply into the spirit's glowing eyes, and the ghost of Blackbeard gazing down at the empty hole where Mara Strega's heart should have n.

"Mara Strega?" the spectral figure asked. "Is it really you?"

"Indeed it is, Edward," the sea witch replied.

"I am but a shadow of the man I once was," the spirit said. "I owe an apology Mara Strega. When I was mortal, I looked to the sea for nture and to piracy for wealth. I did not see how valuable you were. I only say that I am sorry."

"I forgive you, Edward. Farewell my love. May you rest in peace," Strega said, and then the ghost of Blackbeard faded away into the t.

As everyone watched the ghost of Blackbeard fade away, a loud ping sound could be heard inside the treasure chest Rusty Buckles olding. Rusty opened the lid and saw a bright red beating heart.

"Mara Strega! Your heart is beating!" Rusty shouted.

The sea witch reached into the chest and took the beating heart into her hands. She held it to her chest, and it filled the space that had been empty for so long.

"I am whole again!" the sea witch exclaimed. "I now have a heart and am able to remove the curse and return Jonathan to his wife, Rusty. I mean Charlotte."

"Rusty is fine," the lady pirate replied. "Charlotte is who I once was. Rusty is who I am now, a lady pirate with a family made up of pirat and parrots and a sanctuary to help take care of."

The sun rising in the eastern sky began to replace the dark night, and all the pirates and all the parrots felt happy.

"Come everyone. Form a circle," commanded Mara Strega. "'Tis new day, so open your minds and your hearts and believe that the curse will be lifted."

As all the pirates and all the parrots stood facing each other in a circle, the sea witch began to unravel the spell.

"Light is love, and love is light! Shine bright, sun! Remove the night! As the darkness leaves this place, let us see a husband's face! Cur be gone, curse be banished! Let the distance between Rusty and Jonath vanish!"

Once Mara Strega spoke those words, the sound of footsteps co be heard in the distance.

"Who goes there!" shouted the sea witch.

"Fear not," replied a male voice. "I am but a lost and weary wanderer seeking my way home."

A man stepped into view who looked very familiar to Rusty.

"Jonathan! Jonathan!" Rusty cried. "Is it you? 'Tis I, your wife, ιarlotte! Welcome home, Jonathan!"

As if no time had passed at all, the couple fell into each other's ns.

After introductions were made and explanations offered, Jonathan ᴠ just how kind the pirates were, so he decided to become a pirate too ḷ join his beloved Rusty Buckles at the sanctuary to lend a helping hand.

Captain Waylay Wayne and the pirates began preparing for their rney home to the Cape Fear Parrot Sanctuary.

Captain Dogfish Briggins and his parrot Tova decided that they ᴜld travel inland and to the west to help people better understand how ᴐortant it is to for parrots to receive proper care.

Commodore Red knew that there were many more parrots in need ᴏve and care in the land of flowers, La Florida, so he and his parrot Rio ᴀded to **chart a course** south.

Mara Strega, the sea witch, was given a skiff by one of the pirates so she could return home to the Crystal Coast.

Charlie and Tova knew it was time to say farewell.

"Thank you for your friendship Tova," Charlie said to the beautiful bird. "You made me realize just how special I am and that I don't ᴅ to worry about how I look."

"Oh Charlie," giggled Tova, "you are the most talented parrot I ᴇ ever met. I will always love you."

"Wha… what?" Charlie stammered.

"I will always love you!" Tova called as she took flight toward ᴀin Dogfish Briggins who was packed and ready to **venture** west.

34

"Farewell my love! May fair winds bring us together again!" Charl replied. Charlie then climbed up the **rigging,** perched atop the crow's ne on Captain Waylay Wayne's ship, and watched as Captain Dogfish Brigg and Tova walked westward and faded off into the distance. Tova was ou of his sight, but she would always remain in his heart.

Captain Dogfish Briggins and Tova

Epilogue

In eastern North Carolina, not far from the Cape Fear River, the
pe Fear Parrot Sanctuary is home to hundreds of parrot species.
stled safely in the countryside near the Carolina coast, sanctuary
idents live in large-scale aviaries where they fly free and live out their
ural lives in flocks. They eat well, they get the medical care that they
d, they are loved, and they have plenty of human visitors with whom
y love to communicate. And to this day, they are still very good friends
h pirates.

Glossary

Abduct/Abducted: to take; taken

Ablaze: burning, on fire

Adventuresome: bold, daring, adventurous

Ahoy: nautical term to greet someone or call to attention

Aloft: overhead, up in the air

Altercation: a disagreement or fight

Amazon (parrot): a medium-sized parrot native to South Amer Mexico and the Caribbean, mostly green in color

Amuse/Amused: to entertain; to be entertained

Apparition: a ghost

Avast: stop! pay attention!

Aviaries: really big birdhouses

Aye: yes

Bosun: short for "boatswain," one who maintains a ship

Bow: the front of a ship

Brigands: a gang

Capture/Captive: to take someone prisoner; to be held prisoner

st off: untie a ship so it can move out to sea

art a course: to plan a path for sea travel using a nautical map

uldron: a big, black pot used for cooking

ak: to cover; also a cape that is worn as a coat

ckatiel: an Australian parrot

lonies: 18th century term for the United States of America

mb/Combing: to search

ncur: agree

ure: a type of long-tailed parrot

w's Nest: a place near the top of a mast used to keep watch

iously: wanting to know or learn something

rency: system of money

t: money that is owed

ctable: delicious

art/Departure: to leave; leaving

tination: a place someone is going to

ct/Detection: discover; the act of discovering

tion: loyalty

Disembark: to leave a ship

Eclectus: certain parrots of the southwest Pacific with males usually gre in color

Embark: to get on, go aboard, or to begin

Entreat: ask someone to do something

Exclaim/Exclaimed: to suddenly cry out

Expedition: a journey with a purpose to find something

Fer: Pirate speak for "for"

Flatter: to praise someone, to please someone with complimentary statements

Flock: a group of birds

Foe: enemy

Foliage: plant life

Formidable: inspiring respect; appearing capable

Furiously: with much intensity or energy

Gaze: look

Gleam/Gleaming: to shine brightly; shining brightly

Glee/Gleeful: happy; full of happiness

Glimpse: a brief look at something

overnor: the political leader of a state

ammock: a bed made of canvas supported by ropes

arsh: disagreeable

esitation: pause, delay

oist: to raise a flag using ropes and pulleys

orizon: the line where the earth and the sky meet

uzzah: an old word used to express delight, a form of "hurray"

uminate/Illuminated: to light up; to be lit up

deed: certainly; for sure

erfere: prevent something from coming out the way it should

midate: to make someone do something by force, but not usually ysical force

ade/Invader: to enter without permission; one who enters without mission

r Roger: pirates' flag with a skull and crossbones

d ho: an announcement that land can be seen ahead

enant: 18th century word for lieutenant; a junior officer

end: someone or something historically famous

er: to stay in one place a while

Macaw: large, brightly colored parrot of South or Central America

Majority: the greater number

Mast: upright post on a ship that holds a sail

Mate: a member of a crew; also means friend

Mend: to fix something broken, to sew

Merchant: a person who sells things

Morn: Short for morning

Multitude: a large number of

Nary: old word meaning "not"

Negotiate: to discuss a deal

Nestle/Nestled: to be in a place of comfort

Notorious: being well-known for doing something bad

Oblivious: unaware

Observed: saw; watched

Onyx: a beautiful black stone

Pardon: the act of forgiving someone for misdeeds

Peer/Peering: to look/be looking at something very carefully

rch: noun: a branch a bird sits on; verb: to sit on something

ethora: a whole bunch

ach/Poached: to illegally steal an animal; to have stolen an animal

rt: a town with a harbor where ships come and go

ofit/Profitable: amount earned; when money is made

osper: to be financially successful, to have money

ovisions: supplies

est: a search for something in particular

veal/Revealed: to make known; to have made known

ging: the system of ropes on a ship used to support masts and to trol sails

ctuary: a place of safety

ttlebutt: originally a cask (barrel) aboard a ship that contained water, now means gossip or rumors

sail: hoist sails to prepare a ship for departure

nties: types of songs sailors sang while working aboard a ship; Shanty ong

ek/Shrieked: high-pitched expression of terror; to have let out a -pitched scream or expression of terror

ere/Sincerely: to have or to show honest, genuine feelings

Skiff: a small rowboat usually attached to a larger ship that is used to trav from the larger ship to shore

Sloop: a sailboat usually with only one mast

Smitten: overwhelmed by feelings of love
Specter/Spectral: a ghost, a spirit; like a ghost

Spyglass: a small telescope

Squint: to partially close eyes to see something more clearly

Superior: high in status or rank; situated above

Suspicious: not trusting someone

Swoop/Swooped: to move downward through the air/past tense of swoop

Tempest: a windy and violent storm

Thievery: the act of being a thief, the act of stealing

Thorough: complete, detailed

'Tis: old form of "it is"

Toil/Toiling: to work very hard

Topsail: a sail on the top of a mast on a ship (pronounced top-sul)

Torrential: falling rapidly in large amounts

Transfixed: to be motionless and stare at something in fear or amazer

ansport: to take people or things from one place to another

emble: to shake

ove: a collection of valuable things

was: an old form of "it was"

obstructed/Obstruct/Obstruction: to get in the way of; something t is getting in the way; un- not (not getting in the way)

ssel: a ship or watercraft

w: a promise, an oath

yage: a long journey

ylay: to intercept or stop someone in their tracks

yward: headstrong, disobedient

gh/Weighed Anchor: raise an anchor; to have raised an anchor

darm: a horizontal timber attached to the mast

an old form of "you"

how some pirates say "your"

Bibliography for Glossary

Merriam-Webster's Dictionary of English Usage. Merriam-Webster,

Incorporated, 1994.

Dear, I. C. B., and Peter Kemp, editors. *Oxford Companion to Ships and the*

Sea, 2nd ed., Oxford University Press, 2007, *Oxford Reference*,

doi:10.1093/acref/9780199205684.001.0001.

Oxford English Dictionary Online, 2018. www.oed.com.

About the Author

Anna Maria Sophia Cancelli is a coastal North Carolina college glish Instructor and Fund Raising Coordinator for the Cape Fear Parrot ictuary. She enjoys helping parrots and is grateful for her pirate friends o are always at the ready to help the fine feathered residents of the ictuary.

Anna Maria Sophia is more than happy to make appearances at ools, libraries, and museums for readings, and she may even be able to ster a crew of pirates and parrots featured in this story to join her for icational purposes.

Made in the USA
Middletown, DE
03 December 2018